Ladybird  Readers

Spring is Here!

Picture words

Pinkie Pie

Applejack

Fluttershy

Rarity

Rainbow Dash

Twilight Sparkle

Spike

the mayor

ice

wings

ice skates

skate

nest

snakes

Twilight Sparkle jumped
from her bed.

"Wake up, Spike!" she said.
"It's the end of winter."

"Spring must come soon,
and the ponies must help!"

The mayor was in the town with the ponies.

"There are lots of jobs to do," she said. "First, we must take these big clouds from the sky. Then, the birds can come home."

Rainbow Dash and her ponies had wings, and they could fly to the clouds.

But Twilight Sparkle did not have wings.

"Pinkie Pie, you must break the ice with your skates," said the mayor.

Pinkie Pie put on her ice skates.

"I love skating!" she said.

Twilight tried to skate, too.

"Oh no!" she said.

"Some ponies must take the snow from the grass," said the mayor.

"I can help," said Applejack. "I need lots of strong ponies."

"I can do that!" said Twilight.

Twilight tried to take the snow from the grass, but she could not do it.

"Fluttershy must wake the little animals for spring," said the mayor. "Rarity, you can make new nests for the birds."

"I can help Fluttershy wake the little animals," said Twilight Sparkle.

"Oh no! Snakes!"

Then, Twilight tried to make a nest.

"I'm not good at making nests," she said, sadly.

17

Twilight did not have
a job. She felt very sad
because she could not
help the ponies.

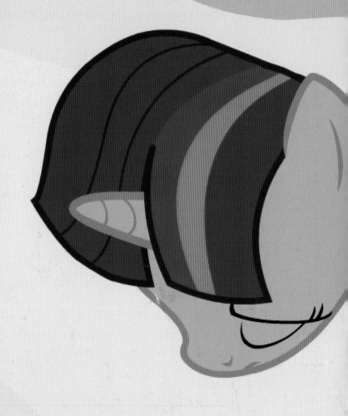

Twilight watched the ponies do their jobs.

"Spring must come soon," she said. "But they are working very slowly."

Soon, the ponies were angry and tired.

"We must move the snow quickly!" said Applejack.

"No! You can't move the snow quickly," said Fluttershy. "We mustn't frighten the little animals!"

"What's the problem?"
said the mayor.

"There's no problem here," said Twilight. "I can help you, but you must all work together!"

"First, help your friends to build nests and wake the little animals," said Twilight.

"Then, you can break the ice
and take the snow from the
grass together!"

Soon, the town was ready for spring.

"Thank you for helping today, Twilight," said the mayor. "You can help us every spring!"

Activities

The key below describes the skills practiced in each activity.

Spelling and writing

Reading

Speaking

Critical thinking

Preparation for the Cambridge Young Learners Exams

1 Look and read. Put a ☑ or a ☒ in the boxes. 📖 🌼

 1 These are ice skates. ✓

 2 This is Rarity.

 3 These are wings.

 4 This is a nest.

 5 This is Rainbow Dash.

31

2 **Look and read. Choose the correct words and write them on the lines.**

Pinkie Pie   Twilight Sparkle   Rainbow Dash   Applejack

1 Her body is purple and her hair is purple and pink.

Twilight Sparkle

2 Her body is pink and her eyes are blue.

3 Her body is orange and her hair is yellow

4 Her body is blue and her hair has got many colors.

3 Find the words.

spring
mayor
wings
snow
skate

ijmspringkrtawingsoltybfeskateepahlmayorjyctfsnowl

Look and read. Write *yes* or *no*.

Twilight Sparkle jumped from her bed.

"Wake up, Spike!" she said. "It's the end of winter."

"Spring must come soon, and the ponies must help!"

6

7

1 Twilight Sparkle stayed in bed. ...... no ......

2 She said, "Wake up, Spike!" ....

3 It was the end of spring. ....

4 The ponies must help. ....

5 Circle the correct words.

The mayor was in the town with the ponies.

"There are lots of jobs to do," she said. "First, we must take these big clouds from the sky. Then, the birds can come home."

8

Rainbow Dash and her ponies had wings, and they could fly to the clouds.

But Twilight Sparkle did not have wings.

9

1 First, they had to take the
(**clouds**)/ **games** from the sky.

2 Then, the **birds** / **clouds**
could come home.

3 Rainbow Dash
had / **didn't have** wings.

4 The ponies could
fly / **sky** to the clouds.

5 Twilight did not have
wings. / ears.

Write the correct form of the verbs.

"Pinkie Pie, you must break the ice with your skates," said the mayor.

Pinkie Pie put on her ice skates.

"I love skating!" she said.

Twilight tried to skate, too.

"Oh no!" she said.

10

11

1 "Pinkie Pie, you must ___break___ **(break)** the ice with your skates."

2 Pinkie Pie ___put___ **(put)** on her ice skates.

3 Twilight ___tried___ **(try)** to skate, too.

4 "Oh no!" she ___said___ **(say)**.

7 Write *could* or *couldn't*.

1  Pinkie Pie

_____could_____ skate.

2  Twilight Sparkle

_____ skate.

3  This pony _____
take the snow from
the grass.

4  Twilight _____
take the snow from
the grass.

8 Circle the correct pictures.

1 What does Rainbow Dash take from the sky?

 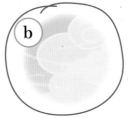

2 Who can move the snow?

3 Who does Fluttershy wake up?

4 Who are the nests for?

9 **Work with a friend. Ask and answer the questions about the story.**

"Fluttershy must wake the little animals for spring," said the mayor. "Rarity, you can make new nests for the birds."

"I can help Fluttershy wake the little animals," said Twilight Sparkle.

"Oh no! Snakes!"

14

15

1 *What must Fluttershy do?*

She must wake up the little animals.

2 Does Twilight want to help Fluttershy wake up the little animals?

3 Can Twilight wake up the little animals? Why? / Why not?

4 What must Rarity make?

10 **Look at the letters. Write the words.** 📖 ✏️ ⭐

1 (i g s w n)

Rainbow Dash and her ponies had .... *wings.* ....

2 (e i c)

"Pinkie Pie, you must break the .... with your skates."

3 (t e s n s)

"Rarity can make new .... for the birds."

4 (S k n a e s)

"I can help," said Twilight. "Oh no! .... !"

11 **Order the story. Write 1—5.**

.... Twilight did not have a job.

.... She felt sad because she could not help the ponies.

____1____ "Rarity, you can make new nests for the birds."

.... "I'm not good at making nests," she said, sadly.

.... Twilight tried to make a nest.

12 Who said this?

Applejack   the mayor   Twilight   Pinkie Pie

1 "What's the problem?"   <u>the mayor</u>

2 "Spring must come
   soon, but they are
   working very slowly." ....

3 "I need lots of
   strong ponies." ....

4 "I love skating!" ....

13 **Read the questions.**
Write complete answers.

1 What is Twilight doing in the picture?

She is watching the ponies.

2 Is it winter or spring?

_____

3 How many ponies are in
the picture?

_____

4 What jobs must the ponies do?

_____

_____

_____

14 **Choose the correct words and write them on the lines.**

---

sadly   strong   fast   slowly   together

1 "Spring must come soon, but they are working very
_____slowly_____," said Twilight.

2 "I can help," said Applejack. "I need lots of _____ ponies."

3 "I'm not good at making nests," Twilight said, _____.

4 Rainbow Dash's ponies could fly _____.

5 "I can help you, but you must all work _____."

15 **Work with a friend. Ask and answer the questions about the picture.** 💬 ❓

1 How did Twilight help spring to come?

She helped the ponies work together.

2 What was the problem before Twilight helped them?

3 Do you like spring or winter best? Why?

16 Do the crossword.

```
1
S
2
n  e  s  t  s
   o
3        4
   w  i  n  g  s
         i
         c
         e
```

Down

1 Strong ponies take this from the grass.

4 Pinkie Pie breaks this with her skates.

Across

2 Rarity makes these for the birds.

3 Rainbow Dash can fly because she has these.

17 **Match the two parts of the sentences.**

1 Twilight woke up Spike because

2 The ponies moved the clouds to help

3 The ponies must take the snow

4 The ponies must make new nests for

5 The ponies must wake up

a the little animals.

b the birds.

c it was the end of winter.

d the birds come home.

e from the grass.

Level 2

The Gingerbread Man
978-0-241-25442-4

Sly Fox and Red Hen
978–0–241–25443–1

The Monster Next Door
978-0-241-25444-8

Wild Animals
978-0-241-25445-5

Little Red Riding Hood
978-0-241-25446-2

Dinosaurs
978-0-241-25447-9

Topsy and Tim The Big Race
978–0–241–25448–6

Goes to the Treehouse
978-0-241-25449-3

Sports Day
978-0-241-26222-1

Going on a Picnic
978-0-241-26221-4

Peter Rabbit and the Angry Owl
978–0–241–28369–1

Superhero Max
978–0–241–28368–4

We Can Help!
978–0–241–28367–7

Daddy Pig's New Van
978–0–241–28371–4

School Trip
978–0–241–28372–1

The Peter Rabbit Club
978-0-241-29811-4

Daddy Pig's Office
978-0-241-29814-5

Spring is Here!
978-0-241-29809-1

Great Trains
978-0-241-29808-4

Hungry Animals
978-0-241-29844-2

Now you're ready for Level 3!